This book belongs to:

The SORE LOSER
(DON'T BE ONE!)

Written by Nia Mya Reese
Illustrated by DG

ACKNOWLEDGMENTS
First, I would like to thank God for giving me the creativity and wits to be able to do this! Thanks to my mom, dad, and my brother (once again) for giving me the inspiration to write this book.

I would also like to thank Mrs. Beth Hankins, my first grade teacher, for helping me put my thoughts on paper. Last, but not least, I want to thank the super people at my church, Faith Chapel, for helping me to not become a sore loser myself.

Love,
Nia Mya

DEDICATION

This book is dedicated to my little brother, Ronald, who teaches me so many life lessons (without getting paid), and to my parents for encouraging me along this crazy/fun ride as an author.

This story is about an 8-year-old girl named Melody. She seems to be a cheerful, nice and normal girl (on the surface). But Melody used to have a problem—she didn't have any friends. Why? Because she was a SORE LOSER.

Whenever she WON, she would brag and bragand brag. She even bragged to strangers, and they didn't even care! But when she LOST, she would have a really BAD attitude.

For instance, after school Melody always runs errands for her mom. Whenever she had a winning day, she used to skip to the store and cheerfully scoot along each aisle, looking for the ingredients her mom needed. She got every single thing on the shopping list. She then opened her book bag and pulled out the money wrapped in a paper with the words "SHOPPING MONEY."

Then she danced along to the checkout and cheerfully said to the cashier,
"Hi, Mr.Todd. Are you having a nice day?" Well, that was if she had WON that day.

On the days she didn't win, Melody stormed inside the store, looked at her shopping list and sighed. Then she stomped up and down each aisle to get what was on the list, and after she was done, she walked to the checkout and sighed again.

When Mr. Todd asked, "Did you win the race today?" Melody just looked at him, raised her voice and said, "NO, IT'S NOT FAIR!" Mr. Todd then told her,

"Well you don't always have to win." But Melody always answered, "YES I DO! I AM A WINNER, NOT A LOSER!"

And there were other times she liked to win—like when her class had a SPELLING BEE. Usually, in the evenings, when she picked up the newspaper for her dad, if she had won, she skipped to the newspaper stand and took the money that said "NEWSPAPER MONEY" out of her book bag.

She dumped the money onto the counter, and Mr. Brown, the person who sells the newspapers, handed the newspaper to Melody and said "I'll bet you had a good day today." Melody answered, "Yes, I won the SPELLING BEE today!" Then she skipped home—but that was only if she had WON.

But if one of her friends, like Jamie or Evelyn, won the SPELLING BEE, Melody stormed to the newspaper stand, opened up her book bag and pulled out the money.

When Mr. Brown asked, "Did you win today, Melody?" (knowing that because of her attitude, she didn't) she shouted angrily and said, "I DIDN'T!" Then she just grabbed the newspaper and headed home.

Although people like Mr. Todd and Mr. Brown tried in a nice way to let her know she shouldn't have an attitude when she loses, Melody was not a very good listener. In fact, she was the worst.

Melody has always loved to play HIDE AND SEEK with her friends. Of course, she loves to win. If she said, "I won today. I'm the best, right?" her friends just sighed. Then Melody would use her chalk to write "WINNER" in big pink letters on the sidewalk. Whenever kids saw a smile on Melody's face, they got very quiet and just went away—because they knew that she would go on and on, bragging and bragging.

Melody didn't even notice when her friends left because she was so happy, she didn't bother to even look up or listen.

On the days that she lost, Melody just sat and glared. The other kids just laughed happily and played without her.

Then one day, it looked like a change was about to happen... Melody's mom had a worried look on her face. This was strange because her mom usually never had that look. But her mom finally realized that Melody's bad attitude had gone on too long.

"MELODY," she called. Melody ran into the living room, smiling from ear to ear because she had just won a game of TIC TAC TOE that she was playing with her sister, Marie.

Melody's mom put her hands on Melody's shoulders and gave her a soft, but very firm look and said, "You need to STOP this behavior."

Melody looked at her and asked, "What behavior?" Melody's mom changed her soft and firm look to just a firm look and said, "You need to stop this behavior of disrespect and self-centeredness. You are a sore loser AND you are not a very nice winner."

Melody's face grew red with anger. When her face was finally the brightest red it could be, Melody yelled, "I AM A WINNER—NOT A LOSER AND I DO NOT HAVE A BAD ATTITUDE! YOU ARE JUST JEALOUS—JUST PLAIN JEALOUS!"

Melody's mom grabbed her and carried her into her room. "This has to stop!" said Melody's mom as she left the room and shut the door. "It has to! This is NOT the behavior I want my little girl to have."

Melody was filled with anger. "They just don't see how GREAT I am!" Melody said, as angry as ever.

A few minutes later, Melody got bored so she looked out the window. What she saw was a group of squirrels playing with acorns.

Each squirrel was busy making its own little pile of acorns. But there was one squirrel that ended up with the biggest pile of all. Melody loved this squirrel because it looked like this one was winning.

But when another squirrel tried to take some of the acorns, the bossy squirrel started jumping up and down, shaking her tail at the other squirrels. They all ran away, leaving the angry little squirrel all alone.

"I know how you feel, little squirrel," Melody said. People just don't see how GREAT we are. People don't want to play with me, either. The bossy squirrel looked like she was listening.
"But I really wish they WOULD play with me," Melody said sadly.

Melody continued to talk to the little squirrel. "I guess if we want more people to stop and play with us, we should be less mad, not focus on ourselves, and have a better attitude—WHETHER WE WIN OR LOSE. I guess what my mom said was true. Maybe if I listened to her, I would have more friends, too."

Melody lifted her head, a little more confident now. The squirrel was smiling as she scampered away. Melody felt better. She felt BRAND NEW. She really did want to work on being less self-centered. She vowed to try to be different.

"Bye bye, old Melody," she said in a singsong voice.

Melody went downstairs and apologized to her parents and sister for the way she had been acting. They were all happy. They loved the NEW MELODY.

Now Melody is on a new mission to be less self-centered. From now on, she will smile. She will congratulate others who win. People might not buy it at first, but as she continues to show a good attitude, whether she wins or loses, people will see that she has changed.

She will begin to make more friends. In fact, she will never be friendless again. Oh, and she will never be dog-less again either, because she got a new puppy because of her good behavior!

NIA MYA'S BIG TIPS!

This is a heads up—that if you brag and boast (and stuff like that), people WILL (I mean like there is a 99% chance they will) find you annoying and rude.

Try to be humble and kind
(like the song, Humble and Kind).
You should really listen to it—search for it.

This all comes back to treating people the way you want to be treated. You need to think of how you would feel if somebody was bragging to you. I don't think that feels good—if it does, then OK, whatever floats YOUR boat.

Remember—however you treat others always comes back to you, good or bad.

ABOUT THE AUTHOR

Nia Mya Reese is an elementary school student who became a best-selling author at the age of 8. Her journey began after a class assignment to write about something in which she was an expert, went viral. Her best-seller, "How To Deal With and Care For Your Annoying Little Brother," attracted both national and international attention. Nia Mya was featured on media airways across the country and around the world, including The Harry Connick Jr. Show, CBS Evening News, Scholastic Classroom Magazine, The Khaleej Times (in Dubai), The Today Show and RTL German TV. She released her second book, "Bully At School: A Bully's Perspective" in 2017. Her stories all have universal themes of finding patience, kindness and love.

Nia Mya continues to ignite the passion for learning in other children during her "Meet The Author" days. Her message to them is twofold: You each have unique gifts, skills and talent, and you are never too young to "FOLLOW YOUR DREAMS."

Nia Mya is an educational product of the Hoover City School System, The Learning Center at New Life, Faith Chapel, and above all, her supportive family. She has a younger brother, Ronald Michael, and is the dearly loved daughter of Ronald and Cherinita Reese.

Stay connected with Nia Mya on social media:
@NiaMyaReese

Other books by Nia Mya Reese:
"How To Deal With and Care For Your Annoying Little Brother"
"Bully At School"

(Books can be purchased on Amazon, Barnes and Noble, and most online bookstores)

Made in the USA
Columbia, SC
22 November 2020

25164851R00022